UFO
on the
Rez

Book One

The Lighthouse Company

Mike Hamel

UFO on the Rez

Published by EMT Communications, LLC
1529 Chutney Court
Colorado Springs, CO 80907
emtcom@comcast.net

First printing—August, 2012

Cover design and illustration, and Interior design and production: Jeff Lane/Brandango.us

You can follow Mike's blog at
www.mikehamel.wordpress.com

To Susan, the light of my life,
and countless others.

Books by Mike Hamel

Matterhorn the Brave series:
The Sword and the Flute
Talis Hunters
Pyramid Scheme
Jewel Heist
Dragon's Tale
Rylan the Renegade
Tunguska Event
The Book of Stories
www.MatterhornTheBrave.com

TLC series:
UFO on the Rez
Bezer's Billions
The Long Walk Home
www.TLCstories.com

Stumbling Toward Heaven: Mike Hamel on Can-
cer, Crashes and Questions
www.StumblingTowardHeaven.com

Table of Contents

1

Zack's UFO

—◊—

Is this another one of your jokes, Zackary Fox?" I could tell from Emma Porter's voice she thought so. Our Thursday morning TLC meeting had barely started and already the members were arguing.

"No joke," Zack said. "I saw a UFO last night." He put one hand on his heart and raised the other as if saying the pledge of allegiance.

Emma rolled her blue eyes.

"You're like the boy who cried wolf," Betti Ryan said. "No one believes you anymore. And put your arm down. You have BO."

Zack sniffed his armpit. "I do not."

Betti's brother, Manny, waved his hand in front

of his nose. He didn't trust Zack either. He'd been tricked too many times.

All of us had.

Zack's my best friend, but what can I say? He's a practical joker.

Two weeks ago at a church picnic, he put spicy cayenne pepper on the potato salad. It looked like paprika. No one noticed—until it was too late. Several folks got steamed over the hot dish. Deputy Longfoot said he couldn't taste anything for three days. He almost wrote Zack a ticket for assaulting a police officer.

"Tell us the story again," I said to Zack. "Slower this time."

He took a deep breath. "My dad and I were stargazing in his canoe last night when all of a sudden something swooshed high above us."

"A plane, maybe?"

"It didn't sound like a plane. It just sort of hummed." Zack hummed through tight lips. "But that's not all." He paused for effect.

Manny couldn't help being curious. "What happened next?"

"The UFO stopped dead and came back," Zack said in a low voice. "It didn't turn. It backed up like a car. It hovered overhead for a few seconds"—pause—"and then"—another pause—"shot straight up into the sky!" Zack shouted this last part and jabbed his hand at the ceiling.

Everyone jumped.

"You're lucky they didn't grab you," Manny said. "I saw a TV show about people who have been beamed aboard alien spaceships and probed with—"

"My brother will believe anything," Betti interrupted. "But he's only eight."

Manny is the youngest member of TLC. TLC stands for The Lighthouse Company. (Don't call us a club.) We meet in the basement of the Cape Myra lighthouse where my Grandpa Tyler is the keeper. People around here call him Captain. It's not a nickname; he earned the rank in the Coast Guard.

People call me JJ. Only my parents call me Jason—and only when they're angry.

"Argyle believes me," Zack said. "Look, he's

wagging his tail."

Argyle, an Alaskan Malamute, is the oldest member of TLC. He's forty-three in dog years and weighs as much as I do.

Zack's pleading gaze moved from Argyle to me. "I'm not lying, JJ."

I nodded and said, "Maybe we should report this to SETI."

"Who's SETI?" Zack wanted to know.

Manny wasn't the only one who watched TV. I knew about SETI from a program on the Discovery Channel. "SETI stands for 'Search for Extraterrestrial Intelligence,'" I explained. "It's a group of scientists who listen for signals from outer space." I brought SETI up as a test. I didn't think Zack would carry a prank that far.

Sure enough, he protested.

"I–I can't do that," Zack stammered. "Dad told me not to say anything. I shouldn't even have told you guys."

"Why doesn't he want anyone to know?" Emma asked.

"Duh," Zack said, circling his right ear with his

index finger. "People will think we're nuts, just like those weirdos Manny saw on TV. You can't tell anybody. Promise."

"Why would we tell anyone?" Betti said. "We don't believe it ourselves."

"Maybe this will convince you." Zack pulled a small round object from his pocket and tossed it on the table.

2

Hard Proof

—⧉—

TLC uses a large wire spool with a plywood top as a table. Its six feet across. Zack's "proof" rolled smoothly from his side to mine. I picked up the dull green thing and rested it in my palm. It looked like the cap off a shampoo bottle, only a lot heavier. "What's this?" I asked.

"That's what I'd like to know," Zack said. "It fell into the canoe when the UFO took off. I bet it's some sort of space metal."

"Let me see," Manny said.

"In a minute." With the blade of my pocketknife I scraped at the dark coating. It didn't scratch.

Next, I pulled out the clear plastic blade I used as a magnifying glass and studied the cap. Its surface was as smooth and hard as steel.

I shrugged and handed the cap to Manny. "TLC has a real mystery to solve."

"But UFOs aren't real," Emma said.

"Zack saw *something*," I replied. "He has hard evidence."

"This?" Betti said as she grabbed the cap from Manny. "Who knows where Zack got it? He could have picked it out of the trash."

"It fell off the UFO!" Zack insisted.

"Or maybe this is like the Indian arrowheads you 'found' last year." She put air quotes around the word "found."

Zack had made the arrowheads out of Play-Doh and hardened them in the oven. The trick had fooled his classmates but not his teacher.

Zack leaned toward Betti and said, "I'll swear to it on a Bible if you want."

He's a joker, but Zack wouldn't take a lie that far. I held up my hand, "Okay. You *did* see something. And we'll help you find out what it was."

"How will we do that?" Emma asked.

"First, we'll check with the CMP," I said. "Maybe others have reported seeing something strange last night."

CMP stands for the Cape Myra Police.

I like to use initials. Get used to it.

"We can talk to Chief Rivers on our way home," Betti offered. She and Manny lived in Cape Myra. Their dad was the pastor of the only church in town.

"I'll ask my folks if they heard any weird stories this morning," Emma said. Her parents owned Scoops Ice Cream Shoppe. Lots of locals and tourists stopped there for coffee.

"Good," I said. "We'll meet at Scoops this afternoon to report what we find. Don't say anything to anybody about UFOs. Keep this on the QT." That's our code word for QuieT.

"What about me?" Zack asked.

"You and I are going to scout the area where you saw the UFO. Maybe something else fell off."

"But we were on the water."

"So we'll check the land nearby," I said. "Do

you know which direction the plane—"

"It wasn't a plane!"

"Okay, the 'craft' headed?"

"West," Zack said.

That meant out to sea. But still, I wanted to have a look around.

As we got up to leave, I took the cap from Betti. Zack held out his hand for it but I said, "There's someone I want to show this to."

"You just said we'd keep it on the QT," Zack protested.

"I know, but I want my grandpa to see this when he gets home."

Zack frowned. "Why show it to him?"

"Because he has friends at the Neah Bay Coast Guard Station."

"So?"

"The station has radar. If anything was in the sky last night, they'll know about it."

"Smart thinking," Zack said.

I touched my temple and said, "It's what I do."

I may only be ten years old but I know a few things about solving mysteries. I've learned them from my mom. She's a security expert, one of the best in the world. The FBI and the CIA have her on speed dial.

"Collect all the facts before reaching a conclusion," she always says.

I believed the facts would lead to a down-to-earth explanation for Zack's UFO. We just had to find it.

3

Lost Boy

—⁓—

It was crisp and sunny outside as Zack and I
hopped on our bikes and headed toward his
place. Argyle tagged along. He wouldn't be
much help in our search. Alaskan Malamutes are
sled dogs, not trackers.

Zack rode an old red Schwinn cruiser with fat
tires, big seat and a missing back fender. I had a
BMX bike, which stands for bicycle motocross. It
had a chrome frame, twenty-inch wheels, knobby
tires and high handlebars.

Zack and I are as different as our bikes. He has
the dark hair and serious face of a Makah Indian.
I'm fair-haired and light-skinned. Zack's eyes are

almost black; mine are brown. He grew up in the woods on the tip of Washington's Olympic Peninsula. I'm a city kid from the other Washington—D.C. We couldn't get any farther apart and still be on the same continent.

Zack lives here year-round. I come every summer. My mom does security work for the government. My dad's a college professor. They travel abroad from June through August. My older sister goes with them. I stay with my grandpa at the Cape Myra lighthouse.

Two summers ago, Zack and I started TLC to solve mysteries, find missing items and help keep an eye on things around town. Today we skirted Cape Myra using the old logging road to get to Zack's place. Suddenly, Argyle got a spurt of energy and ran ahead. I pedaled after him and saw an old shoe poking out from behind a rotten log.

Zack came up next to me and asked, "What is it?"

"Just some litter," I said.

But when Argyle took the dirty sneaker in his mouth, we heard a loud "*Yeow!*"

UFO on the Rez

A skinny Mexican boy in torn clothes sat up and crawled backward like a crab. He probably thought he was being attacked by a wolf. Argyle looks a lot like his wild cousins.

"It's okay," I called. "He won't hurt you."

The kid stared up at me as I walked over. He didn't look so good. He had a purple eye above a swollen left cheek. The front of his yellow shirt had red spots from a bloody nose.

He didn't smell so good, either.

I reached down to help him up.

He jerked away from my hand.

I went back and got the water bottle from the clip on my bike. "My name's JJ," I said as I offered it to the kid. "What happened to you?"

The boy didn't answer; he just eyeballed the bottle. Finally, he took it and sat on the log. After a long drink, he wiped his mouth on his sleeve.

"Where's your bike?" Zack asked.

The boy shrugged his shoulders.

"How'd you get out here?

Another shrug.

"Do you speak English?" I asked.

No reply.

Zack was getting upset. The boy needed help but obviously didn't want any. After another minute of awkward silence, Zack said, "We can't stay here all day, JJ. Remember our, er, business."

I patted my bike seat and said to the boy, "Hop on. I'll take you to town. "You can call your folks from the police station."

His eyes got wide at the word "police." "*No!*" he cried.

So he did know some English. "We can't just leave you here," I said.

He stared at the ground and said nothing.

Finally Zack said, "It's a free country," and rode away.

The kid tried to return my water bottle but I waved it off. "I live at the lighthouse," I told him. "Bring it back when you're done with it."

I pedaled after Zack, not expecting to see the bottle, or the boy, again.

4

Detective Work

—◦◦◦—

We made it to Zack's house in time for lunch. The Foxes own three acres on the Strait of Juan de Fuca. Zack put his finger to his lips as we went inside to remind me not to say anything. His mom didn't know about the UFO.

After some tomato soup and sandwiches, we put on our life vests and climbed into Zack's canoe. He and his dad had carved it out of a cedar tree. Argyle came too. Like me, he enjoys being on the water. Unlike me, he's a good swimmer.

Zack handled the canoe like a pro, paddling to the spot where he and his dad had seen the UFO.

I had hoped the water would be shallow enough to see shiny objects on the bottom. No such luck. I lifted my eyes to the closest land—a narrow strip of sand hemmed in by tall trees.

"Might as well check the shore," I said.

"We're not going to find anything, are we?" Zack said as we beached the canoe.

"Probably not," I admitted. "But we have to look. It's part of good detective work." I took a handheld metal detector from my pack and began sweeping the sand. It was one of the gadgets I'd brought to the lighthouse that summer. Over the next half-hour we did find a few things—bottle caps, fishing lures, even a seal skull—but nothing like the piece from the UFO.

We paddled back to Zack's and then pedaled to town. We racked our bikes in the gravel parking lot behind Scoops. The gang waited at our special table. Because Emma's parents owned the place, we got treated like VIPs—Very Important People.

Scoops has everything a kid could want. Clear plastic bins of candies and nuts for sale by the ounce. Glazed donuts delivered fresh daily. Malts so thick you had to chew them. And kindly owners who lived by the Golden Rule. The words were even carved into a five-foot-long plaque hanging in the center of the back wall.

"DO UNTO OTHERS AS YOU WOULD HAVE THEM DO UNTO YOU."

Mrs. Porter greeted us from behind the L-shaped counter and began fixing TLC milkshakes for Zack and me. We had invented the special drink last summer. It's a top secret recipe involving lots of chocolate. That's all I can say.

Mr. Porter took a water bowl and dog chew outside for Argyle.

"Did you learn anything from the CMP?" I asked Betti.

"No reports of strange sightings last night," she said.

"Your mom or dad hear anything?" I asked Emma.

"No," she said over the top of her frosty glass. "What did you and Zack find?"

"Nothing," I replied.

"That's not true," Zack said. He turned his chair around and draped his arms over the back. He leaned in and whispered, "We found a body in the woods."

Betti scoffed, "First a UFO, now a body."

"We found a *boy*," I said as everyone looked to me for the truth.

Zack cracked a smile. "He had a body, didn't he?"

Emma flicked her straw at Zack. He tried to lick the chocolate off his cheek but his tongue wouldn't reach.

Some milkshake also got on Manny. Gray whiskers and a pink nose popped out of his shirt pocket. It was Wilbur, his pet rat, trying to get at the sweet stain.

"Down boy," Manny said, putting his hand over his pocket.

"Argyle found a Mexican boy by the logging road," I explained. "The poor kid looked like someone beat him up."

"Where is he now?" Betti asked with concern.

Zack shrugged. "Still there, I suppose."

"You just left him!" Emma cried.

"He wouldn't budge," Zack said.

"We have to go back and find him!" Betti practically shouted.

"Find who?" asked the big man sitting at the coffee bar.

5

Angus Keaton

—⚍—

Chief Rivers of the CMP brought his cup over to our table and sat down. The Chief is a Makah Indian with a broad face, wide shoulders and thick arms. He is soft spoken and hard headed. He used to be an MP, a Military Policeman. You do *not* want to get on the wrong side of the law in Cape Myra.

"JJ and I saw a Mexican kid in the woods," Zack told the Chief. "He was hurt but wouldn't let us help him."

"Probably a farm worker," the Chief said. "They pretty much keep to themselves."

"He's a long way from home," I said.

"They come up to Whatcom County to pick strawberries every year," the Chief said. He pointed east with his chin. "Sometimes if the work is slow, a few wander down to the Rez looking for work."

The Rez is short for the Makah Indian Reservation. It occupies the most northwestern part of the US. Look it up on a map.

"But why would this boy be all alone?" Emma asked the Chief.

"Good question," he replied. "I'll drive out to the migrant camp and see if anyone's—"

"There you are," a booming voice interrupted.

Angus Keaton strode down the main aisle, his boots leaving dirt waffles on the polished oak floor. Angus was a jack-of-all-trades. He had done everything from prospecting to fur trapping to commercial fishing up and down the West Coast. He had more tall tales than Pecos Bill.

Angus nodded at us and then bellowed at the Chief, "I've got a burglary to report!" Angus doesn't have an inside voice.

"What was taken?" the Chief asked.

"My reading glasses," Angus said, pulling a chair over to our already crowded table.

I saw the Chief hide a smile behind his coffee cup.

"And my gold pocket watch," Angus went on. "It belonged to my dad."

"Maybe you just misplaced them," the Chief suggested.

"Hello, Angus," Mrs. Porter called over. "Would you like some coffee?"

Angus nodded. "Black as a coal miner's lungs."

"Did you check under the couch cushions?" the Chief asked.

"I've searched my place from top to bottom," Angus said. "It ain't that big."

Angus lived in an old homesteader's cabin out by Seal Rock. He had never married and had no family but he collected animals like a sweater collects lint. At last count he had nine cats, five dogs, two goats, a pot-bellied pig and a rooster with a harem of chickens. He even had a llama.

Chief Rivers put his cup down and asked, "What do you want me to do?"

"Catch the thief!"

When the Chief didn't say anything, Angus growled, "I've got a shotgun. I'll use it if the burglar comes back."

"That gun's older than you are. It's liable to blow up in your face. Besides, you can't shoot someone over glasses and a watch." Then the Chief got an idea. "TLC might be able to help," he said with a nod toward me.

"What's this bunch got to do with my problem?" Angus asked.

"TLC solves mysteries and finds stuff," I said.

Angus narrowed his blue eyes at me and rubbed his stubbly chin. "How much does TLC charge?"

Zack's face lit up at the thought of money. I gave him an elbow before he could say anything. "We don't charge for our services," I said.

"Well, the price is right. You're hired."

When Mrs. Porter brought his coffee, Angus reached for his wallet. "Don't worry about it," she said. "I'll put it on TLC's tab."

"We have a tab?" Zack said. "In that case—"

"Milkshakes are the only thing you get." Mrs.

Porter extended the coffee toward Angus.

Angus reached for the cup and knocked over Emma's glass.

That's when Wilbur made his move.

6

Chocolate Rat

—⚉—

anny's pet rat jumped out of his pocket and landed on all four paws, tail up and whiskers twitching. He scrambled into the sticky mess and started licking. Wilbur loves chocolate.

Mrs. Porter screamed at the rodent's sudden appearance and dropped the coffee cup.

Chief Rivers rocked back to keep from getting burned. Zack wasn't as fast. He yelped as the hot liquid splashed on his arm.

Manny grabbed for Wilbur and knocked the milkshake glass off the table.

Emma fell sideways off her chair.

All this excitement scared the poop out of poor Wilbur. Literally. He left a trail of droppings as he raced around the table looking for a way down.

I used my empty glass to trap Wilbur. The bit of chocolate on the bottom dripped on him like brown rain. He stood on his hind legs, snoot in the air, pink tongue slurping the gooey goodness. He was in rat heaven.

Chief Rivers laughed at all the fuss but Mrs. Porter was not amused.

"Manny Ryan!" she scolded in that voice all moms have. "Get that rat out of here before I toss you both to the cats!"

I slid the glass to the edge of the table. Manny cupped his hands and caught Wilbur. "Sorry Mrs. Porter," he mumbled.

Emma picked herself up and said, "Rats are gross. Where'd you ever get the idea to have one for a pet?"

I know exactly where Manny got the idea.

From me.

Last summer I'd told him about King, my hooded rat. King was smart and I had taught him to do tricks like run a maze and roll around inside a plastic ball. One morning I lost him while playing on my bed. Without thinking, I shook the blanket. King flew high into the air and came down on his little hood.

Too bad it wasn't a helmet.

That was the end of King.

"Hooded rats make great pets," I said in Manny's defense. "They're very clean and easy to train."

"Then train that one to stay out of my shop," Mrs. Porter snapped.

Everyone rose to leave. I told Angus we would come out to his place tomorrow to study the crime scene and look for clues. Zack offered to help Emma clean up the mess. I offered to help Manny wash Wilbur.

I went outside with Manny and Betti and we walked to Cape Myra Church where their dad is the pastor. The Ryans live next door in the white house with the wraparound porch. Pastor and Mrs. Ryan had adopted Betti and Manny from Ethiopia when they were very young. Their birth names were Bethlehem and Emanuel, which the Ryans shortened. The family had lived in Seattle until

Mrs. Ryan had been killed in a car crash. They moved to Cape Myra four years ago.

As we approached, I saw Pastor Ryan on the porch swing. His moustache and beard matched his short auburn hair. He kept in great shape and even competed in triathlons. Looking up from his book, he asked, "What happened to you, son?"

Manny muttered something about chocolate and went inside. Betti sat next to her dad and started explaining. I followed Manny and helped give Wilbur a bath in the kitchen sink. Then I put him in his yellow plastic cage while Manny washed and put on a clean shirt.

We returned to the porch where I plopped into the wicker chair with the purple cushion. Emma had finished with Wilbur's adventure and was telling her dad about the boy in the woods. "I hope Chief Rivers can find him," she said.

"He may not want to be found," Pastor Ryan replied.

"Why not?"

"Because if he's here illegally, he'll be sent home."

7

Fugitivo

—⟋⟍—

That evening, I had KP after supper. KP is military slang for Kitchen Patrol. Through the window above the sink I saw something out by the trees. I opened the door to go check just as Argyle came running around the lighthouse. He reached the spot before me and growled at the stranger hiding in the shadows.

I recognized the Mexican kid from the woods, his brown eyes wide with fright. He had my water bottle in his shaking hands.

"Argyle won't bite," I assured him.

"I–I return this," he said with a heavy accent.

"Thanks." I took the bottle. As he turned to leave, I asked, "Have you had dinner? There's some spaghetti left."

I watched the struggle on his face. His mind said "leave" but his stomach growled "eat." In the end, his stomach won.

A minute later, he sat at the kitchen table and I stood at the microwave warming the spaghetti. I added a slice of garlic bread and put the plate before him. He bowed his head and said a silent grace.

I poured him a glass of milk, then sat down and watched him dive in. "What's your name?"

"Juan," he said through a mouthful of pasta.

"I'm JJ," I said. "Where are you from?"

"A small village near Manzanillo, Mexico." He pronounced the *x* like an *h*.

"Are you a farm worker?"

A quick nod. Juan was about my height but skinnier than me. His thick hair was a few shades darker than his skin. Neither had been washed in some time.

"You seem kind of young to be working in the

fields," I said.

Juan wiped his chin with a napkin. "I am eleven. This is my third time here." He held up three fingers with crescents of dirt under the nails. "Uncle Carlos brings me."

"Where are your parents?" I asked.

"*Muerto*," Juan said softly. When he saw I didn't understand, he said, "Dead."

"I'm sorry." To change the subject, I asked, "What were you doing in the woods today?"

"Hiding from Miguel."

"Who's Miguel?"

"The crew boss. He hits me."

"So you ran away?"

"I am looking for my uncle. He is missing."

"Missing?"

"Since Monday." Juan cleaned his plate with the bread and I got him another piece.

"That's three days ago. You should tell the police."

"No. Uncle Carlos has our papers. Without them, I will be sent back."

"Chief Rivers is the law here. He can help."

"You maybe," Juan sneered. "You are *gringo*."

"The Chief isn't like that," I replied. "Come to think of it, he isn't a *gringo* either. He's a Makah Indian."

A look of hope crossed Juan's tired face. "Will you ask him?"

"First thing in the morning," I promised.

He pushed his empty plate away and stood.

"Do you need a ride to the worker's camp?" I asked.

"I cannot return without my uncle," Juan said. "Miguel will beat me. Perhaps I will go missing too."

That sounded bad. "Then you can sleep here," I offered.

Juan glanced out the window. "I want no trouble for you. If Miguel finds out . . ."

"It's no trouble."

"*Gracias!*" Juan sighed with relief. I could tell he didn't want to spend the night alone outdoors.

"No problemo," I said. "Let's go see a man about a bed."

8

Ockham's Razor

—◠◠◠◠—

We climbed the eight-story lighthouse tower to the lower deck where we found Grandpa reading. I introduced Juan and told his story. Grandpa asked Juan several questions in Spanish. After a few minutes of talking he said, "You're welcome to stay, Juan. Tomorrow we'll see about finding your uncle."

"*Muchas gracias*," Juan said with relief.

We went downstairs and I finished the dishes while Juan took a shower. He cleaned up nicely, except for the bruise on his cheek.

I loaned him some PJs and my sleeping bag,

which he rolled out on the living room couch. "You like puzzles?" he asked, eyeing the table littered with jigsaw pieces. The box showed a beautiful tropical island floating in a royal blue sea.

"That's Grandpa's," I said. Before I could show Juan the 3-D cityscape puzzle I was doing in my bedroom, he pulled up a folding chair and started working on the island.

Since I wasn't allowed to touch Grandpa's puzzles I climbed the tower again. Grandpa was still in his favorite canvas chair, stocking feet on the rail, reading glasses balanced on the tip of his nose, open Bible in his lap. He'd been at Cape Myra since retiring from the USCG, the United States Coast Guard, that is. Grandma had gone to heaven two years before that and Grandpa lived alone, except for Argyle. I made it a threesome in the summertime.

Our Grand Lady—that's what Grandpa calls the place—is one of the twenty-seven lighthouses in Washington. She fills the gap between the Cape Flattery and Skip Point lighthouses. She's almost ninety feet tall. Her tower is white with a gray crown. Inside is a lantern room atop a service room.

UFO on the Rez

I love it up here: the gentle breeze full of sea smells; the sky turning indigo above the trees. It was a clear night and the light hadn't come on yet. As in most modern lighthouses, it was triggered by a light-sensitive switch.

I unfolded a chair next to him and asked, "What will happen to Juan?"

"That depends on whether his uncle can be found," Grandpa said. "If not, Chief Rivers will have to call the INS."

"What's that?"

"The Immigration and Naturalization Service," Grandpa said. "It's the outfit that keeps an eye on—"

Suddenly, a dark blur shot overhead like a giant shell fired from an unseen cannon. It left a ripple of air in its wake.

I blinked my eyes and gasped. "Did you see that!"

Grandpa pushed his glasses up his nose and nodded.

I jumped up and headed toward the stairs.

"Where are you going?" Grandpa asked.

"To get my night vision goggles in case that thing

43

comes back."

"It won't," Grandpa said with certainty.

I returned to my chair. "Was that a UFO?"

"No," Grandpa said.

"Are you sure? Zack saw one last night. He even has proof." With all the excitement over Juan, I had forgotten about the strange cap until now. I took it out of my pocket and handed it to Grandpa.

He palmed the dark green metal and smiled. "You ever hear of Ockham's Razor?"

"No," I said. "Is it some kind of knife?"

Grandpa shook his head. "William Ockham was an English monk who lived a long time ago. He believed that the simplest explanation for a mystery was usually the right one."

I puzzled over what Grandpa meant.

"There's a simpler explanation than a UFO for what we just saw," Grandpa went on. "And as for this . . ." He held up the cap.

"You know what it is?" I asked.

"Not exactly," Grandpa said. "But I know some-one who might."

9

The Comanche

—⁓—

Bright and early Friday morning we took
Juan to the CMP. Chief Rivers and Deputy
Longfoot listened quietly as Juan told about
his missing Uncle Carlos. Grandpa translated the
parts Juan couldn't put into English. The group of
migrants they worked with had been in the area
a few weeks picking strawberries. As often happened, Juan and his uncle wound up on different
crews on Monday morning. Carlos didn't return to
camp that night.

"Miguel would not look for him," Juan said.
"He does not like my uncle."

"Miguel is the crew boss," I spoke up. "He's the

one who hit Juan."

The Chief scowled. "Let's drive out to your camp and talk to this Miguel."

"He will be *muy enojado*. Very angry." Juan shifted from foot to foot.

I could tell he was afraid, so I said, "Can Juan stay with me until his uncle turns up?"

"That might be safer for now," the Chief agreed.

"Is that okay with you?" I asked Grandpa.

He nodded to the Chief and said, "We'll stop by on our way home to learn what you find out. We've got other fish to fry this morning."

Before we left, Deputy Longfoot drew a sketch of Carlos based on Juan's description. He's a pretty good artist. The deputy, not Juan.

We drove west to Station Neah Bay, the USCG base in Neah Bay. It's one of two units in the Thirteenth Coast Guard District. Juan had never seen anything like it. So we gave him a quick tour, driving past the helicopter refueling pad and the boat house.

In-dock we saw a forty-one-foot UTB—Utility

Boat—and a couple of forty-seven-foot MLBs—
Motor Life Boats. They had been used in the re-
cent capture of some eagle poachers. I smiled as I
remembered TLC's part in the case.

The SC—Station Chief—greeted us warmly
and invited us into his office. Commander Dodd
and Grandpa had served together a long time ago.
I introduced Juan, who nodded but said nothing.

"What brings you down from your tower?" the
Commander asked.

Grandpa tossed the dark green metal cap onto
the desk.

Commander Dodd picked it up and said,
"Where'd you get this?"

"It fell into Zack Fox's canoe the other night,"
Grandpa said.

"Zack thinks it came off a UFO," I added.

"What do you think?" the Commander asked
me.

I shrugged.

Grandpa scratched his forehead with the bill of
his cap. "I'd say a stealth helicopter."

The Commander's eyebrows rose.

"No doubt the same bird that buzzed the lighthouse last night," Grandpa said.

"You saw it?"

"We heard it," Grandpa corrected. "And if it keeps zipping up and down the Strait, everyone on the coast will know about it."

Commander Dodd sighed. "The chopper is no longer top secret," he said. "No harm in showing you." He typed a few words into his computer and turned the monitor. The screen showed a sleek helicopter with a built-in tail rotor.

"The Comanche is one of the most advanced helos in the world," Commander Dodd said. He scrolled down to the specs and I began reading aloud. "The Boeing Sikorsky RAH-66 Comanche can travel at 175 knots an hour. It can make snap turns, fly sideways or backwards or climb straight up at a rate of 1,418 feet per minute."

"What's it doing in Neah Bay, besides scaring the locals?" Grandpa asked,

"It's part of the Army's Force XXI Plan," Commander Dodd said. "But that program has been cut. The Coast Guard is thinking about buying this one from the Army. We've been putting it through its paces the past few nights."

"The Comanche has a three-barreled nose gun that fires 1,500 rounds per minute," I kept reading. "It can carry up to fourteen Hellfire anti-tank missiles and deploy up to twenty-eight Stinger air-to-air missiles."

Grandpa smiled. "Expecting an invasion?"

"Most of those weapons have been stripped off," Commander Dodd said. "We'll use it for SAR." SAR is short for Search and Rescue.

"Can we see it?" I asked hopefully.

The Commander frowned. "Don't push your luck."

"Then can I get a picture of the Comanche to show Zack?"

"Tell you what," the Commander said, hitting the print key. "I'll trade you a picture for the cap."

10

One Down

—*m*—

By the time we got back to Cape Myra, Chief Rivers had returned from the migrant camp. He'd learned nothing about the missing uncle. Miguel had not been very helpful. None of the other workers would talk at all. They feared Miguel more than they feared the law.

The Chief put out an APB on Uncle Carlos. That stands for All Points Bulletin. It alerted other police departments to keep an eye out for a missing person. "The county sheriff told me of two new camps in the area. I thought I'd check them out this afternoon."

"Is there anyone at the camps you want to stay

UFO on the Rez

with?" Grandpa asked Juan.

"Not a good idea," the Chief said before Juan could answer. "Not without his papers. The camps are checked often for illegals and he would be deported immediately."

I thanked the Chief for not turning Juan in.

"As long as I know where he is," the Chief said.

"With us," Grandpa said, putting a hand on Juan's shoulder.

"Can we get something to drink before we go home?" I asked when we walked outside.

"I'll fuel the van and pick up you in fifteen minutes," Grandpa said.

I steered Juan toward Scoops and found Zack and Emma at our usual table. I could hardly wait to tell them about the UFO, but first I introduced Juan and explained his situation.

"Sorry for leaving you in the woods," Zack said. "I'm glad you're okay."

"You have the same name as the Strait," Emma said as she brought us two Cokes.

This confused Juan.

"The Strait of Juan de Fuca," she explained. "The water between here and Canada."

The mention of Canada gave Zack an idea and he said to Juan, "Chief Rivers will find your uncle. He's like the Canadian Mounties; he always gets his man. Dead or alive."

Emma kicked him under the table for that last part.

Time for a change of topic. I pulled out the picture of the helicopter and unfolded it on the table. "Here's your UFO, Zack."

His eyes got wide.

"This is the Comanche," I went on. "The Coast Guard has been flying it around the last few nights."

"Dad will be glad to see this," Zack said. "Can I have it?"

"It's yours. I had to trade the metal cap for it."

"Mystery solved," Emma said.

"TLC still has two other cases," I reminded her. "Finding Juan's uncle and Angus's burglar."

Mr. Porter stuck his head out of the back room and asked his daughter, "Are you coming with me to Forks?"

Forks is forty miles south down Highway 101. It's the nearest town of any size—not big enough for a Walmart but much larger than Cape Myra. It has a several motels and restaurants, a few gas stations, a library and a hospital. This is why I said to Emma, "You should go. Tell your dad about Carlos. See if you can check the hospital for a Mexican Juan Doe."

"And if I find one?" Emma asked.

"Call Chief Rivers." I turned to Zack and said, "Go get Betti and Manny and meet us at the lighthouse. We're going for a ride."

11

Crime Scene

—⁓—

Zack, Betti and Manny showed up at three o'clock sharp. Juan had fallen asleep on the couch and I left him there. I hopped on my bike and we rode out to the dirt road that snakes through the woods between Seal Rock and Snow Creek. We found the mailbox with "Angus Keaton" in faded white letters on the side and followed a narrow footpath to the old cabin.

Angus sat rocking on the porch. His dogs began barking as we got near but the sight of Argyle kept them at a distance. The barking set the chickens to clucking and flapping around like ... chickens. The rooster crowed as if the sun had come up.

"About time you got here!" Angus hollered.

We dropped our bikes in the clearing in front of the cabin. A goat came over and started nibbling on Zack's padded seat.

"Get away from there!" Zack yelled.

"You do *not* want to do that," I warned the frisky animal.

Angus got up and said, "C'mon, Recycle." He took the goat by the collar and clipped it to a chain wrapped around a tree. He rattled the chain and smiled. "She chews through anything."

"Why'd you name your goat Recycle?" Manny asked.

"Because that's what she does."

No sooner had Angus secured the first goat than a second one came around the corner. This one had a beard and horns. The billy goat saw Zack bent over checking his bike seat and drew a bead on Zack's rear end.

"Hazmat!" Angus yelled as the billy lowered his head and charged.

Zack jumped out of the way just in time. The goat crashed into the bike and went sprawling.

Angus picked up the animal by the horns and said, "Mind your manners, Hazmat. These are guests." To Zack he said, "Never tempt a goat like that unless you don't want to sit down for a week."

"You would be the butt of our jokes for twice that long," I said.

Everyone laughed, even Zack.

"Hazmat sounds Arabian," Betti said.

"It's short for hazardous materials," Angus said as he hooked Hazmat next to Recycle.

"Mind if we look around?" I asked.

"Knock yourselves out."

Trees crowded around the cabin on three sides. The open windows had gingham curtains flapping in them. The back door wasn't locked. When I asked about this, Angus scoffed. "If I wanted to lock my doors, I'd move to Seattle."

As we followed him inside, he said, "The original log cabin was built in 1914. Over the years it's grown to four rooms. I added the electricity and plumbing myself."

"Then what's that for?" Manny asked, looking

out the window at an old outhouse.

"Emergencies," Angus said.

The living room had hunting and fishing magazines piled everywhere. Used paper plates littered the tan carpet. Soda-can totem poles stood at both ends of an orange plaid sofa. A tabby cat sprawled in an overstuffed chair covered in the same ugly fabric.

Manny patted his empty shirt pocket. Good thing he'd left Wilbur at home.

The bedroom was even messier and smelled like a gym locker. Dirty clothes draped over every surface. The rumpled bedspread looked like an old horse blanket.

"A good house cleaning should solve this case," Betti whispered.

"Are you volunteering?" I whispered back.

She quickly shook her head.

"What did you say was missing?" Betti asked as the five of us crowded in.

"Not missing," Angus said. "Stolen."

She shrugged. "What's been stolen?"

"My gold pocket watch, my glasses and half a

cherry pie got filched two nights ago."

"Were you home?" I asked.

"Sleepin' right there." He pointed to the un-made bed.

"And you didn't hear anything?"

Zack frowned. "How could anybody sneak up on this place with the racket your animals make?"

"Easy," Angus said. "I snore like a chain saw."

I could read the doubt on the others' faces as we went to the kitchen. I suspected if Angus had really been robbed, that's where we would find the proof.

12

Mrs. Claus

—⟨⟨⟨—

I spotted an empty pie tin on the kitchen counter. There were red stains on it and bits of crust on the floor. Angus's poor housekeeping had given us our first break. "You said the burglar ate half a cherry pie?"

Angus nodded.

I carefully put the unwashed tin in the plastic bag I'd brought for evidence. Chief Rivers could dust it for fingerprints. I also bagged a glass and two forks from the sink.

"JJ is big on detective work," Zack told Angus. "He likes to find clues and figure things out. Thinks he's a regular Sherlock Holmes."

I pretended to take a pipe out of my mouth and said with a British accent, "Come, Watson. The game is afoot!"

We went back outside and spent half an hour searching for footprints or other signs of a human presence. Nothing.

"I'll let you know if we turn up any fingerprints," I told Angus as we got on our bikes. "Does anybody else live nearby?"

"There's the Young place down the road," he said. "It was their summer getaway for many years. When George died, his widow sold their house in Phoenix and moved here."

Manny perked up. "Mrs. Young teaches my Sunday school class. She's cool."

"Maybe she saw or heard something the other night," Zack said.

"Let's go see," I said.

The seventy-foot mobile home was easy to find. Mrs. Young greeted us at the door. She looked like a chocolate Mrs. Santa Claus. She was a well-padded black grandma with full cheeks, round chin and wire-rimmed glasses.

After inviting us in, she asked, "What brings the famous TLC to Seal Rock?"

"You've heard of us?" Zack said innocently. Everyone in Cape Myra had heard of TLC, but he was fishing for a little praise.

"It's all Manny talks about in Sunday school," Mrs. Young said.

This was Manny's first summer in TLC. It was the greatest thrill of his eight-year-old life.

Mrs. Young went into the kitchen and returned with a plate of sugar cookies. "I heard about what you did for Avi and the orphans at Galich," she said. "Very nice of you."

She was referring to the suitcase of Skittles we'd sent to Russia, but that's a different story.

"Angus had some things stolen a few nights ago," I said as I took a cookie. "We're checking into it. Did you see or hear anything unusual Wednesday evening?"

"No," she said with concern. "What was taken?"

"His watch and glasses," Betti said.

"You call that a crime?"

The question came from the hallway. The speaker was a tall, dark-skinned teen with corn-row hair. He wore a New York Knicks basketball jersey and shorts that hung to below his knees.

"Everyone," Mrs. Young said, "this is my grandson Terrell. He's staying with me for a few weeks."

"Hi, Terrell. I'm JJ." I introduced the rest of TLC.

Terrell looked at Zack and asked, "Are you a real Indian or a half breed?"

Zack bristled. "I'm a full-blooded Makah. My people have been on this land for centuries."

"My people," Terrell smirked.

"Don't be rude, Terrell," his grandma scolded.

He shrugged and leaned against the wall, arms folded across his chest.

"Terrell is from New Jersey," Mrs. Young said. "This is his first time in the Pacific Northwest."

"More like Pacific Nothing," Terrell said. "What do you do here all day? Play cowboys and Indians?"

"That's enough," Mrs. Young said. "You might

not be so crabby if you got out and did a few things." She nodded at me and said, "JJ lives in a lighthouse. Maybe he would give you a tour if you asked politely."

"Not interested," Terrell said as he turned and walked away.

13

Trailer Stash

—⁓—

I apologize for Terrell's behavior," Mrs. Young said after he retreated to his room. "He's going through a hard time and his mother thought a change of scenery would do him good."

"If Terrell changes his mind about the lighthouse, I'd be happy to show him around."

"Thank you, JJ," Mrs. Young said. "If I can get him to church on Sunday perhaps you could invite him again."

"Sounds like a plan." I stood to leave. "You might want to lock your doors until the thief is caught."

"Call Chief Rivers if you see anyone suspicious,"

Betti added.

"Yes, dear."

"Why'd you offer to show Terrell around?" Zack asked after we got outside. "He's a real jerk."

"Maybe he's nicer when you get to know him," I said. "Besides, it sounds like he could use some cheering up."

We climbed on our bikes and I whistled for Argyle. He pawed at a piece of trailer skirting that had come loose. "C'mon boy."

Argyle had excellent hearing but he ignored me. I coasted over to see what was so interesting. The sunlight over my shoulder glinted off something shiny under the trailer.

I dropped my bike and got on my knees. I reached in with two fingers, plucked out the round object and dropped it into my pocket. "Great work, Argyle," I said, scratching his broad head.

I didn't say anything to the others until we reached the road. I stopped and showed them the gold watch.

"Will you look at that," Zack said, staring as if at a hypnotist's watch.

"How did that get under Mrs. Young's trailer?" Betti asked.

"She can't be a crook," Manny said, defending his teacher.

"Relax, Manny," I said. "If Mrs. Young stole this, she would've taken it inside."

Zack jumped to a conclusion and announced, "Terrell's the thief."

"Just because he's rude doesn't mean he's a robber," Betti said.

It's not like there are a ton of suspects who live here," Zack said, holding up two fingers. Then he put one down and said, "And Manny's right about Mrs. Young not being a crook."

"We could have Chief Rivers check for prints," Betti suggested.

I put the watch in the plastic bag with the pie tin. "Terrell's too young to have prints on file unless he's been in juvenile hall."

"He probably has," Zack said. "Did you see his gangsta hairdo?"

"You can't judge a book by its cover."

"What you see is what you get," Zack said.

"First impressions can be deceiving."

"Idle hands are the devil's tools."

"Never trust a—"

"Enough with the sayings," Betti interrupted. "Let's just go back and talk to Mrs. Young."

I shook my head. "She doesn't know anything or she would have told us. Besides, I've got a better idea."

Zack leaned over his handlebars. "What's your plan?"

"A stakeout."

"No way will our parents let us spend the night out here," Betti said. "Not with a prowler on the loose."

"A video stakeout," I said. "And I've got just the surveillance device we need."

"Surveil—" Manny tried to say.

"Spying," Zack said.

My mom works with the latest high-tech gear and I get some of the older stuff. Some of it I bring to the lighthouse. Among other goodies, my collection includes:

- Two-way wristwatch radios.

• Infrared goggles for seeing at night.

• A GPS locator that shows where you're at anywhere on Earth. GPS stands for Global Positioning System.

• A hand-held metal detector smaller than the ones used at airports.

• A digital video camera that fits in the palm of my hand.

It would do the trick nicely.

14

Candid Camera

—⁓—

As soon as we got back to the lighthouse I grabbed the spy cam and brought it down to TLC headquarters in the basement. Juan was awake and came with me. I passed the sleek silver unit around the wire spool we used as a table.

"Sweet," Zack said as he palmed the tiny camera. It was only three inches long, two-and-a-half inches high and one inch thick.

"It's so small," Betti said.

"It's huge compared to what the pros use," I said.

"Where does it store the video?" Manny asked.

"On this." I slid a special SD card from a slot on the bottom of the camera. SD means Secure Digital, in case you don't know tech lingo. "This card has sixteen GBs of memory. It can hold up to ten hours of low-resolution video."

GB stands for a gigabyte—one million bytes of information.

"How close to the trailer will it have to be?" Betti asked.

"Not very," I said. "It has a ten-power zoom. It also has an LCD—Liquid Crystal Display—flip screen for video playback."

"Can it see in the dark?" Manny wanted to know.

"It doesn't have to," Zack said. "There's a full moon tonight."

"It has a low-light setting," I added.

We spent the next half hour making plans. On their way home, Betti and Manny would take the watch to the CMP, along with the pie tin. Zack and I would ride back to Mrs. Young's at dusk and hide the spy cam. We would all meet at Scoops in the morning to review the video.

My legs ached but I didn't complain as Zack and I pedaled back to Sail River at sundown. We found the perfect spot for the spy cam in some rocks about fifty feet from the trailer.

"Keep down," Zack whispered as we crawled to the rocks. "We don't want Terrell to see us."

I aimed the camera and turned it on, then gave Zack the thumbs up signal.

We rode to Zack's house to get his toothbrush and a change of clothes so he could spend the night at the lighthouse. Zack, Juan and I ate popcorn and played games until eleven o'clock.

—m—

My alarm went off at 6:00 am. I had to peel Zack out of his sleeping bag like a cheese stick out of its wrapper and we hit the road by 6:20.

An early start, but not early enough.

Someone had been up earlier and stolen my spy cam!

We couldn't find any footprints on the rocky ground. No broken twigs on the nearby bushes.

The camera had disappeared into thin air.

Zack pointed to a window on this side of the mobile home. "Wanna bet that's Terrell's room?" he said. "He must have seen us last night."

"Only one way to find out," I said. That camera cost a lot of money—well, I hadn't actually paid for it—and I wanted it back. I marched toward the trailer, upset enough to pull Terrell out of bed and search his room.

Zack was probably right about Terrill. The kid wasn't just at the top my suspect list. He was the only one on it.

15

Prime Suspect

—⁓—

Despite the early hour, I banged on the metal door. Mrs. Young looked out the little window in the door before answering. She opened the door wearing a long gray housecoat and holding a steaming mug of cinnamon tea.

"What are you doing out so early?" she asked as she invited us in.

I took a deep breath and told her about finding Angus's watch under her trailer yesterday. I explained about the video stakeout and the stolen camera.

The second I finished, Zack pointed down the

hall to the door on the left. "Is that Terrell's bed-room?" he asked.

Mrs. Young set her mug on the coffee table and glared from Zack to me. "I do *not* like being spied upon in my own home," she said with an edge. "Nor do I like my grandson being called a thief." She stood up and ordered, "Show me where you found the watch."

We went outside and I knelt by the loose piece of skirting. I wanted to crawl under the trailer and look for clues but Mrs. Young was in no mood to give permission.

"I'll fix this today," she said. "Tell Chief Rivers about finding the watch and losing your camera. Let him handle things."

My camera had been stolen, not lost, but I decided not to argue. She had a right to be angry. "Sorry about the surveillance," I said. "And about accusing Terrell."

I expected Zack to also apologize but he kept silent.

"I'll talk to Terrell about this," Mrs. Young said. "You would see he's not a bad kid if you got to know him."

"Yes, ma'am," I replied.

—m—

Since we knew Chief River's routine, Zack and I didn't pedal to the police station but went to Scoops instead. Emma let me use the phone to call Grandpa. I asked if he could bring Juan to town.

"There were no Mexicans in the hospital at Folks," Emma said as she brought half a dozen glazed donuts to our table. I filled her in on the Angus burglary and what we'd found at Mrs. Young's trailer.

Chief Rivers came in for his morning coffee at nine o'clock sharp. I repeated the story to him, ending with the theft of my camera.

He scowled at me. "People have a right to their privacy. What you did was illegal."

"It won't happen again," I told the Chief. How could it? My spy cam was gone.

Mrs. Porter brought the Chief his coffee.

"Did you find any fingerprints on the pie tin or

watch?" I asked.

"Only Angus's," Chief Rivers said after a long sip.

"I still think Terrell's the thief," Zack spoke up. "Angus never had anything stolen until he showed up. And where did we find the missing watch? Hidden right under his bedroom." Zack's voice got louder. "Terrell probably saw us set up the camera last night. Then he snuck out and took it. Nobody else knew about it."

The Chief wasn't buying it. "Lots of coincidences, but nothing—"

"Figured I'd find you where the doughnuts were!" Angus walked past the coffee bar and sat down by the Chief. "Don't you ever stay in your office? I always have to track you down when I need you." He took a donut from the plate.

"Can't do police work behind a desk," the Chief replied. Before he could say more, Zack piped up, "We found your watch."

Angus leaned forward and asked, "Where?"

"Under Mrs. Young's trailer."

16

Soccer Star

—w—

The Chief gave Zack a stern look. "I'll do the talking." He turned to Angus. "Mrs. Young's grandson is staying with her. Has the boy been around your place?"

"Twelve- or thirteen-year-old kid?" Angus asked. "Weird hair."

The Chief looked at me and I nodded.

"He's been by a time or two." Angus scratched his chin. "He likes animals."

"Or maybe he was casing the joint," Zack said.

"Enough," the Chief warned.

Angus took a bite of donut and said, "If it's him,

he came back last night. My gold Zippo lighter is gone. It's always on the mantle next to my pipe, but not this morning. Besides that, a box of frosted flakes got spilled all over the counter."

If Terrell was the culprit, my spy cam would have filmed him leaving the trailer and returning with the goods.

All the more reason for him to have taken it.

Chief Rivers said he was going to drive Angus home so he could check out the crime scene. Then he would stop by and talk to Mrs. Young and Terrell.

—⚍—

Grandpa brought Juan to Scoops and, after treating him to a TLC milkshake, Zack, Emma and I gave him the grand tour of Cape Myra. It is west of Port Angeles on Highway 112. Scoops Ice Cream Shoppe sits in the center of town. To the left is the Strait Inn Motel. To the right is Nate's Hardware & Tackle. Keep going and cross the street and you come to the CMP. It's in the front of a one-story brick building. In back is where the volunteer fire department keeps its ancient red fire engine.

On the other side of town is Risto's Gas Station, the last one before reaching the Pacific Ocean.

A block southeast from Scoops is Cape Myra Church. We just have one and it's generic. If you want a special flavor of Christianity you have to drive to Neah Bay or Forks. The Ryans live next door and we stopped to get Betti and Manny.

Behind the church is the town park—a block-square patch of grass with a softball diamond at one end and a small basketball court with one rim at the other. In between is the soccer pitch. That's it. Cape Myra has no public swimming pool, tennis court or health club. Most people here work for exercise.

Juan's spirits perked up when he saw the make-shift soccer goals.

"You play?" Emma asked.

"*Si,*" Juan said.

"Then wait right here," she said, and raced off.

Emma plays for a premier soccer club. She's faster than most boys her age and scores a lot of goals. But when she got back with a ball, it soon became clear Juan was better. He could shoot and pass with either foot. He could play the ball off his chest, shoulders or head. And he ran like a deer.

We weren't the only ones admiring Juan's skills. Down the block, a man sat watching in an old pickup. He flicked his cigarette ash out the window and said quietly, "*Allí usted es.*"

There you are.

17

Stranger Danger

—◦◦◦—

The stranger started to open his door but stopped when Pastor Ryan came over with a pitcher of pink lemonade and a box of energy bars. We sat in the grass and shared the snacks.

Pastor Ryan invited Juan to church and to the picnic afterward. Cape Myra Church hosted a pot-luck in the park every summer Sunday. After the meal came either a softball game or a soccer match. Tomorrow it would be soccer in Juan's honor.

His eyes lit up and he nodded like a bobblehead doll.

Ten minutes later we were using the soccer ball

to shoot baskets when the stranger in the pickup finally got out. He took three steps, turned around and slunk back in as the white-and-green CMP cruiser pulled up courtside.

Chief Rivers called us over to his window. He held out the spy cam and asked me, "This yours?"

"Yes," I said. "Where'd you find it?"

"The same place you found Angus's watch."

"Under Mrs. Young's trailer!" Zack cried.

"His lighter was there too."

"So Terrell's the thief," Zack concluded.

"I didn't say that."

"But he—"

"—spent last night watching TV with his grandmother," the Chief cut Zack off. "She swears he never left the trailer."

Zack said nothing. He didn't think Mrs. Young had lied, but maybe Terrell had slipped out his window after she'd gone to bed.

I reached for my camera and said, "The truth will be in here."

The Chief shook his head. "I already checked. Nothing. I could keep this because it was used in an illegal surveillance you know."

I held my breath.

"But I'll return it to TLC as a professional courtesy." He handed me the camera. "See that it doesn't happen again."

When he drove off, we hurried to Scoops to review the video. It was easier to see the screen inside but there was nothing to see except Mrs. Young's trailer. I fast-forwarded to where the screen blanked out because the camera had been shut off.

"That didn't tell us anything," Emma said.

Zack disagreed. "It tells us the thief snuck up from behind and turned it off, which means he knew where it was. And only Terrell could have seen JJ and me plant it."

"It also tells us no one came out of the trailer," Emma said.

"Unless Terrell snuck out the back way and circled around," Zack replied.

While they argued, I examined my camera more closely. There were thin scratches on the silver casing. They hadn't been there before; I always

take good care of my stuff.
    Those scratches were clues.
    I just had to figure out what they meant.

18

Scratching for Clues

—∽—

The next afternoon we were back at the park for the picnic. Juan had enjoyed church, even though he couldn't understand much of the sermon. He had been warmly welcomed and Pastor Ryan had even given him a Spanish Bible.

Grandpa brought a big pot of his famous Lighthouse Chili. "This will set your lights to flashing," he warned anyone brave enough to try it.

The chili smelled wonderful but packed a real kick. Grandpa stirred it with a big wooden spoon because he said the stuff would melt plastic.

Deputy Longfoot said it would melt the enamel

off your teeth.

Mr. Risto said it could remove oil stains from concrete.

"It needs more *habaneros*," Mr. Porter complained. "I can still feel my tongue."

Children and small animals weren't allowed near the chili. Zack had tried it last year and had ended up in the bathroom the rest of the day.

—ᴍ—

After the meal, we divided into two groups: those who wanted to play soccer and those who wanted to watch. As we had planned yesterday, TLC all ended up on the same team and we chose Juan as our captain. The other team had more adults but it didn't matter. No one could stop Juan and Emma. The black and white ball made a gray blur between their flashing feet.

Still, we only won by two goals. The other team scored twelve times because Zack was our goalie. He only stopped the shots that actually hit him.

Mrs. Young was at the picnic but I avoided her

because I felt guilty about what had happened. My taste buds overcame my conscience when I saw her dishing out homemade ice cream after the match. When I got my bowl of strawberry swirl, she said coldly, "Chief Rivers came by yesterday. He asked to look under my trailer for stolen goods. He even searched Terrell's room. I have never been so embarrassed in my life."

"I'm sorry," I said.

"You should be," she replied. "I had hoped Terrell would make some friends in Cape Myra. I invited him to church and the picnic but he said he didn't want to be around people who think he's a thief."

This made me cringe.

Her expression softened and she said, "But I can't explain how all that stuff got under my home either. Something's going on."

"And TLC will get to the bottom of it," I promised. I sat down and dug into my bowl. In between bites I asked about Terrell. I learned his mom worked two jobs and had three other children. His dad was an Army Ranger and had been overseas for months. The Rangers are an elite military force—look them up.

"Does Terrill like sports?" I asked.

"Not really. He's more into chess and astronomy."

That gave me an idea. "How about if Grandpa and I swing by on our way home and pick up Terrell for some star gazing tonight? There's no better place for it than the Sky Box."

The Sky Box is an old abandoned lookout tower deep in the woods where TLC sometimes meets.

"It's worth a try," Mrs. Young said.

—␣␣␣—

Grandpa agreed, and so did Terrell when we stopped by an hour later. What convinced him was Grandpa's offer to let us use the telescope. Grandpa owned a Celestron AstroMaster 130 EQ that he used to watch both ships and stars.

As we climbed into the van, a glint caught my eye. It was the setting sun reflecting from the loose metal skirting where I'd found Angus's watch. I went over for a closer look. There were thin scratches in the white paint, exposing shiny aluminum. I ran my finger along one of the marks. I didn't remember seeing them the last time.

Grandpa honked.

I slid into the middle seat next to Terrell. After an awkward silence, I said, "I'm sorry we got off on the wrong foot the other day."

"Do you always sic the cops on new kids?" Terrell said.

"The Chief is just doing his job," I said. "I know you didn't have anything to do with the thefts."

This surprised Terrell. "What made you change your mind?"

"Evidence," I said.

19

Trapped in the Tower

—◆◆◆—

On Monday morning, Grandpa drove to Port Angeles to do the grocery shopping. Juan and I slept in. We had stayed up late taking turns at the telescope with Terrell in the Sky Box. What an odd trio: a middle-class white kid; an inner-city black guy; and a Mexican migrant worker. The only thing we had in common was the stars.

Terrell turned out to be a pretty smart kid. He knew the constellations and a lot more. He'd already skipped a grade in school and was taking advanced math and science classes. The more he talked, the more I liked him. And when he asked if he could come to the lighthouse, I said sure.

After a late breakfast Juan and I climbed the lighthouse tower. In the lantern room I explained how the VRB—Vega Rotating Beacon—worked. "It has a metal turret and a six-place lamp-changer with halogen bulb. Every lighthouse has a distinct pattern for its light. Ours flashes white, followed by twelve seconds of darkness. Then it flashes red, followed by another twelve seconds of darkness. Then the cycle repeats."

Juan looked bored.

I started to suggest returning to the house when we heard a distant rumbling. I stepped on deck and saw a tornado of dust coming up the service road. It wasn't Grandpa. He didn't drive that fast.

Juan stood next to me and grabbed my arm. His grip tightened when a beat-up pickup pulled into view. "Miguel!" he cried.

"We'll stay up here," I told Juan. "We can hide in the service room."

I peeked over the rail as the primer-gray truck skidded to a halt. A large man got out and stomped toward the door. His face was brown and wrinkled like an old saddle. He looked mean and angry.

His huge fist pounded on the door.

My puny knees knocked together.

Suddenly, Miguel glanced up and caught me looking down. I ducked back but it was too late.

"I know you are there, *muchacho!*" he yelled. "Where is Juan?"

My heart jumped into my throat.

"Don't make me come up there!" Miguel threatened.

No use trying to hide. I stuck my head over the rail and said in a shaky voice, "Who's Juan?"

"Stop playing games," Miguel snarled. "I saw you together in town."

"Oh, that Juan," I gulped. "He, he isn't here. He left last night."

Miguel pointed his finger at me and shouted, "You lie!"

"He's gone," I repeated. "I don't know where he went."

"I saw you with those church people. Did they teach you to tell lies?"

What could I say to that?

Miguel cursed in Spanish and reached for the door knob. "I'll see for myself!"

"I'll call the police!" I yelled.

Miguel sneered. "You have a phone up there? I think not."

He opened the door but never made it to the stairs.

He never made it into the kitchen.

He barely made it back to his truck in front of Argyle's snapping jaws.

Argyle had been in the living room and at the sight of the stranger had gone off like a stealth rocket.

"Get him!" I shouted from above.

Argyle didn't bark. He almost never does. He just put his massive paws on the truck door and bared his teeth.

Miguel rolled down the window and tried to hit Argyle with the baseball bat he kept under the front seat. But Argyle snatched it away like a puppy playing fetch with a stick. Miguel almost lost a few fingers before he got the window back up.

Then he tried to run over Argyle but only managed to raise a cloud of dust.

At last he gave up and drove away. I suppose he feared Grandpa might return or I would come downstairs to call the police.

And that's exactly what I did.

20

The Exception

—⚬—

Chief Rivers didn't come out to the lighthouse. Instead, he went looking for Miguel at the migrant camp. Grandpa got home an hour later. As we helped carry in the groceries, I told him about Miguel's visit and how Juan and I had hidden in the tower.

Grandpa was upset. "I shouldn't have left you two alone."

"We weren't alone," I said. "Argyle was here. He chased Miguel away."

"JJ protected me," Juan said. "He was *muy valiente*. Very brave."

"I was scared spitless," I admitted. "It made

me do something I'm not proud of." Then I told Grandpa about lying to Miguel.

The Captain has high standards. He won't tolerate lying, disrespect to others, or taking the Lord's name in vain. Just ask those who served with him in the Coast Guard and didn't watch their mouths.

"I know it's wrong," I tried to justify myself. "But Miguel would have taken Juan and beaten him again."

Grandpa put a hand on my shoulder. "It's okay, JJ. Lying is wrong, but in this case I think it was the right thing to do."

This caught me off guard.

He returned to emptying the grocery sacks. "Do you remember the story of Rahab in the Old Testament?"

Grandpa reads his Bible every day and practically has the whole thing memorized.

I recalled the name but couldn't quite place the story.

Grandpa read my puzzled look and frowned. "How about Joshua and the fall of Jericho?"

"Yes."

"Joshua sent two spies into the doomed city and they stayed with a woman named Rahab. When the king's men came looking, she hid the spies and lied to the soldiers. For this, Joshua spared her life and welcomed her family into the nation of Israel. Later on in the Bible this tale is used as an example of faith."

Grandpa opened a box of orange juice and poured himself a glass. After a long drink, he said, "Rahab lied to save those men, not to mention her own skin. You did the same thing today, JJ. You made the best choice in a bad situation."

This made me feel better.

"But make no mistake," Grandpa added. "This is the exception, not the rule. Now finish up here and let's go see the Chief."

Chief Rivers wasn't at the CMP station but Deputy Longfoot said he would be back soon. Grandpa, Juan and I headed to Scoops to wait. Emma, Betti and Manny were at our table in the back.

"Sorry about Wilbur," Manny was saying to Mrs. Porter as we joined them. It was about the tenth time he had apologized over the past few days.

"It's all right," Mrs. Porter said, nodding at me. "JJ tells me hooded rats make fine pets. I hope you have lots of fun with Wilbur. Just not in here."

"When I was a boy," Grandpa said, "I had a pet skunk. She raised quite a stink with the neighbors." He smiled at his own pun.

"You think that's odd?" Mrs. Porter said. "Before Peter and I got married, he had two pet porcupines. You could say that Peter Porter possessed a pair of prickly porcupines."

We all laughed, except Mr. Porter. He had heard this tongue twister too many times before.

I told everyone what had happened at the lighthouse while Mrs. Porter mixed up a batch of TLC milkshakes. A few minutes later Chief Rivers and Zack came in. Between then walked a stranger in a faded cotton shirt, dirty jeans and cowboy boots.

Juan jumped up and cried, "*Tio!*"

21

Uncle Carlos

—⟋m—

Juan and his Uncle Carlos hugged each other and jabbered away in Spanish. Zack plopped down between Emma and me, a smug look on his face. The Chief took a seat at the counter next to Grandpa.

"Where'd you find him?" Grandpa asked, tilting his head toward Juan's uncle.

"Canada."

"How'd he get over there?"

"Ask Zack Fox," the Chief said. "He's the one who tracked him down."

All eyes turned to Zack, who loved being in the spotlight. "Good old detective work," he said with a swagger in his voice. "I got a copy of the sketch Deputy Longfoot made of Carlos and showed it around the Rez. Bill Watah recognized him as the guy he'd paddled over to Canada last Monday. I called Chief Rivers and told him."

At this point the Chief took over the story. "It turns out Miguel sent Carlos across the Strait to buy supplies. Miguel said the exchange rate made things cheaper, but it was a trap. He had secretly stolen Carlos's work papers and phoned the Canadian authorities with a tip about an illegal alien. They picked Carlos up and were in the process of deporting him."

"How'd you get him back into the US?" Mr. Porter asked.

"I called the INS and cleared everything up," the Chief said. "They had his work permit on file."

"But why did Miguel have it in for Carlos?" I asked.

Grandpa translated my question and Carlos's answer. It turns out Miguel had been cheating the workers, keeping back some of their pay. Carlos became suspicious so Miguel wanted him out of the way.

"Are you going to arrest Miguel?" I asked the Chief.

"He already has," Zack spoke up. "You should have seen it. After we picked up Carlos, we drove to the farm where the migrants were working. Miguel lied through his teeth about framing Carlos and hitting Juan. The guy's an idiot."

"You don't have to be mean," Mrs. Porter said.

"Miguel took a swing at the Chief," Zack said.

"Then Miguel *was* an idiot," I said.

Zack nodded. "He was face down and hand-cuffed before he knew what hit him."

I glanced over at Chief Rivers and didn't see a wrinkle or speck of dirt on his khaki uniform.

"We took Miguel straight to Port Angeles," Zack continued. "He'll be deported tomorrow."

The word "deported" brought a big smile to Juan's face. "*Muy bueno*," he beamed. "Very good."

What we didn't know until later is how close all the Mexicans came to being sent home, including

Juan. But the Chief had talked Carlos into taking over as crew boss. He also smoothed things over with the farmer who had hired the migrants to pick strawberries. The owner had not been pleased with their production but agreed to give them a second chance.

The happy reunion lasted another hour. Grandpa and Carlos discovered they had a lot in common. As a Coast Guard Captain, he had been up and down Mexico's Pacific coast from Mazatlan to Huatulco. He had been in the port of Manzanillo many times, which was near the village where Carlos and Juan lived. Grandpa even knew a ham radio operator in Manzanillo and offered to make contact.

Grandpa didn't own a cell phone. There was no service at the lighthouse. He had no interest in Facebook or Twitter, but he stayed in touch with friends around the globe the old fashioned way— by radio. He has been a "ham" for decades. *Ham* is the nickname for amateur radio operators. There are still more than 3 million of them in the world. Look it up.

22
Pilot's Wings

—⁓—

The next evening Juan and his uncle came out to the lighthouse to "phone home." Several of their relatives had been reached by the Manzanillo ham operator. They gathered for the call, which lasted a long time. Afterward, Juan came to a special TLC meeting held in his honor.

"Since you'll be around awhile longer," I said to Juan, "we might as well make you an honorary member of TLC."

We were meeting up on deck, so I sent Zack to the basement for the TLC Seal. It's a special rubber stamp Mrs. Porter made for us. It has a lighthouse with rays shooting from the top and the initials

TLC underneath.

I stamped the back of Juan's hand with the seal and said, "Now, raise your right hand and repeat after me." But before I could start the TLC pledge, I saw something over Juan's shoulder that froze my vocal chords.

The RAH-66 Comanche came zooming out of the night toward the lighthouse, its three-barreled turret gun pointed right at me! The wind from its rotors drove us into the service room as it stopped fifteen feet away! We pressed our faces to the windows in wide-eyed wonder.

With its built-in tail rotor and space-age design, the helicopter seemed like something out of a 3-D video game.

"*Yikes!*" Betti screamed.

"*Awesome!*" Zack yelled.

"*The Comanche!*" I shouted.

The chopper pivoted sideways and rose a few feet. Through the large glass canopy we could see the pilot as he reached over and opened the side window. Then he gave a crisp salute and tossed something onto the deck. The next moment, the

Comanche shot straight up like a yoyo on a 1,000-foot string and disappeared!

Zack ran out and picked up the object. The brick-sized metal box had another box inside. This one was felt-lined and held a pair of shiny pilot's wings. Not a cheap toy but the real deal. There was also a handwritten note, which Zack unfolded and read as we crowded around.

To Zack Fox:

In trade for returning our turbo-shaft cap nut. Sorry about the scare the other night.

The note was unsigned. Zack polished the wings and pinned them to his shirt with pride. "Well, isn't that something," he said. "A Comanche giving a gift to a Makah."

Before I could say anything, he scowled at me and warned, "No wisecracks about Indian givers."

Grandpa and Uncle Carlos came racing upstairs to see about the racket. Juan blurted the story in Spanish while Grandpa scanned the sky. When he lowered his gaze, he spotted the wings on Zack's chest. He smiled and touched the bill of his cap, giving Zack his second salute of the evening.

We got back to Juan's TLC pledge and then continued our meeting. After he left we had another item of business. "The mystery of Zack's UFO has been solved," I said. "Juan and his uncle are safe. We just have one more case to wrap up."

"The Angus burglary," Emma said.

"Which won't be a problem now that we know who the thief is," I said.

"We do?" Manny and Betti said at the same time.

I nodded and held up the picture I had found that afternoon.

23

Masked Bandit

—ᜃ—

On Wednesday morning TLC pedaled out to Angus's cabin. His dogs barked a greeting that scattered the chickens. Angus sat in his rocking chair reading an old issue of *Field and Stream*. He wore a red plaid shirt, torn jeans and unlaced hiking boots.

Zack, Emma, Betti, Manny and I trooped up the steps and sat down on the dusty floor since there were no other chairs on the porch. I noticed the glasses perched on the tip of his nose and said, "I thought your glasses had been stolen?"

"Me, too," Angus said, "but I found 'em behind my night stand."

"JJ figured out who took your other stuff," Emma said.

Angus rocked forward and said, "You know who the burglar is?"

Zack made circles around his eyes with his fingers and said, "It's a masked bandit."

"What are you talking about?" Angus asked.

"A furry felon," Zack said. "A ring-tailed robber. A crook with claws. A thief with—"

"A raccoon," I finally interrupted.

Angus resumed rocking and looked skeptical. "I didn't see any tracks."

"That's because it jumped from a tree through your window," I said. "A raccoon fits all the evidence. It comes out at night. It loves sweet food, which explains the cherry pie and frosted flakes. It likes shiny objects, which is why it took your watch and lighter. And my camera. The scratches on the camera got me on the right track. I found the same marks on the skirting of Mrs. Young's trailer."

"But why cart my stuff that far?" Angus said.

"That's where its den is," I said. "Adult males

roam within a three- to eight-mile area."

Angus scratched his nose. "How'd you know that?"

"I looked it up."

Wanting to show off his own knowledge, Zack said, "Raccoons are members of the bear family and are very strong."

I frowned at this.

"Look it up," he challenged.

I turned back to Angus and said, "Put screens on your windows and I bet the burglaries will stop. Or use a live trap and release the animal elsewhere."

Angus thought this over for a few moments and then said, "In the old days I could've made a coon-skin cap out of the rascal."

"Eeww!" Betti said. "Who wants to wear dead animals on their heads?"

Angus laughed. "Screens aren't a bad idea. Keep out the flies, too."

Just then, Hazmat and Recycle came around the corner looking for brunch. Zack jumped up and ran to protect his bike seat. He waved his arms and yelled, "Scram before I make goat cheese out of you!"

The goats circled him and eyed the other bikes. It was time for us to make like trees and leaf while we still had something to sit on.

"You kids are razor sharp at this detective business," Angus called as we rode away.

"We're TLC!" I yelled over my shoulder. "It's what we do!"

—〰—

List of Initials

BMX – Bicycle Motocross

BO – Body Odor

CMP – Cape Myra Police

GB – Gigabyte

GPS – Global Positioning System

INS – Immigration and Naturalization Service

JJ – Jason Tyler

KP – Kitchen Patrol

LCD – Liquid Crystal Display

MLB – Motor Life Boat

MP – Military Police

SAR – Search and Rescue

SC – Station Chief

SD Card – Secure Digital Card

SETI - Search for Extraterrestrial Intelligence

TLC – The Lighthouse Company

QT – Quiet

UFO – Unidentified Flying Object

USCG – United States Coast Guard

UTB – Utility Boat

VIP – Very Important Person

VRB – Vega Rotating Beacon

Matterhorn the Brave

Matterhorn the Brave™ follows the exploits of four teens recruited by the Praetorians of First Realm—a mirror world of Earth—to keep an eye on the portals connecting all space and time. When heretics murder the king of First Realm, his daughter enlists the kids' help to recover some of the Ten Talis that have been hidden on Earth. The Talis are symbols of the Maker's power. The heretics need these sacred objects for their scheme to conquer Earth.

Each book in this epic adventure is set in a different place and time and features a colorful cast of unique characters.

BOOKS IN THE SERIES:

Book 1 *The Sword and the Flute* – Ireland, AD 700

Book 2 *Talis Hunters* – Pacific Northwest, 10,000 BC

Book 3 *Pyramid Scheme* – Egypt, 1325 BC

Book 4 *Jewel Heist* – Bermuda Triangle, AD 1292

Come visit Matterhorn the Brave at
www.matterhornthebrave.com

TLC – The Lighthouse Company

www.tlcstories.com

The Lighthouse Company (TLC) is a group of kids who meet in the basement of the Cape Myra light-house run by Mr. Tyler, aka The Captain. His grand-son, JJ, comes to live with him every summer and leads TLC in solving mysteries, finding treasures and helping Cape Myra's two-man police force.

BOOKS IN THE SERIES:
UFO on the Rez – Zack Fox has seen a UFO—and he has proof! But while hunting for more clues, he and JJ stumble upon Juan, a young migrant worker who needs to find his missing uncle before Miguel, the evil crew boss, finds Juan.

Bezer's Billions – Did Old Man Bezer leave behind a secret treasure when he died? Will the skeleton key JJ finds in the basement lead to untold riches for TLC or unexpected trouble?

The Long Walk Home – One morning, JJ and Zack

are blown out to sea by a freak storm. When the Coast Guard finds their empty canoe, the search is on to rescue the boys before the dangers in the Olympic forest put a tragic end to their long walk home.

About Mike Hamel

Mike Hamel lives in Colorado, a long way from the Pacific Ocean. He is the father of four grown children, the Papa of six grandchildren and the author of the *Matterhorn the Brave* series (www.MatterhornTheBrave.com). He has also written several books for grownups available on Amazon. He blogs at OPEN Mike, https://mikehamel.wordpress.com.